Short Story Press Presents

Jacklighters

Granddaughter Saves
Grandfather From
Extraterrestrials

Bill Knorr

**Copyright © by Short Story Press
(Owned by Hot Methods)**

**For More Short Stories, Visit
ShortStoryPress.com.**

Thank You

Thanks for getting this book!

Our ULTIMATE goal is to share our short stories to the world! We strongly believe that our publishing company is unique because we focus on unique and original short stories written by everyday people throughout the world. Our short stories are our small way of making a positive impact in the world by entertaining you, our Short Story Press reader to the fullest with our Short Story Press stories.

To help get the word out, your honest reviews and feedback are greatly appreciated. So after you have read this book, we'd like to ask you to take a quick moment to review the book. Thank you and we wish you all the best.

Thank you for your reviews online. We appreciate your honest reviews and feedback online. Thank you for being a Short Story Press reader. For more short stories, visit ShortStoryPress.com.

If you want to check out our non-fiction books, then check out our HowExpert guides at HowExpert.com.

To your success,

BJ Min
Founder & Publisher of Short Story Press
ShortStoryPress.com

Recommended Resources

- www.ShortStoryPress.com – Short Stories Written by Everyday Writers.
- www.HowExpert.com – Quick 'How To' Guides by Everyday Experts.

COPYRIGHT, LEGAL NOTICE AND DISCLAIMER

COPYRIGHT © BY SHORT STORY PRESS (OWNED BY HOT METHODS) ALL RIGHTS RESERVED WORLDWIDE. NO PART OF THIS BOOK MAY BE REPRODUCED, STORED IN A RETRIEVAL SYSTEM, OR TRANSMITTED IN ANY FORM OR BY ANY MEANS - ELECTRONIC, MECHANICAL, PHOTOCOPY, RECORDING, OR OTHER - EXCEPT FOR BRIEF QUOTATIONS IN PRINTED REVIEWS, WITHOUT PRIOR PERMISSION OF THE PUBLISHER.

REPRODUCTION OR TRANSLATION OF ANY PART OF THIS WORK BEYOND THAT PERMITTED BY SECTION 107 OR 108 OF THE 1976 UNITED STATES COPYRIGHT ACT WITHOUT PERMISSION OF THE COPYRIGHT OWNER IS UNLAWFUL. REQUESTS FOR PERMISSION OR FURTHER INFORMATION SHOULD BE ADDRESSED TO THE PUBLISHER.

THIS PUBLICATION IS DESIGNED TO PROVIDE fictional INFORMATION IN REGARD TO THE SUBJECT MATTER COVERED. IT IS SOLD WITH THE UNDERSTANDING THAT THE PUBLISHER DISCLAIMs liability for anything related to the topic or the book. NEITHER THE PUBLISHER NOR AUTHOR SHALL BE LIABLE FOR ANY LOSS OF PROFIT OR OTHER COMMERCIAL DAMAGES, INCLUDING BUT NOT LIMITED TO SPECIAL, INCIDENTAL, CONSEQUENTIAL, OR OTHER DAMAGES.

ANY TRADEMARKS, SERVICE MARKS, PRODUCT NAMES OR NAMED FEATURES ARE ASSUMED TO BE THE PROPERTY OF THEIR RESPECTIVE OWNERS, AND ARE USED ONLY FOR REFERENCE. THERE IS NO IMPLIED ENDORSEMENT IF WE USE ONE OF THESE TERMS.

COPYRIGHT © BY SHORT STORY PRESS (OWNED BY HOT METHODS) ALL RIGHTS RESERVED WORLDWIDE.

Table of Contents

Thank You 2

Recommended Resources 3

Jacklighters 6

About the Writer 25

Thank You 26

Recommended Resources 27

Jacklighters

Len Wilkins lingers after spending the day planting posts for a new fence on the north side of his farm. He places his hands on the small of his back and stretches as he looks with satisfaction on the straight line of fence posts. He massages his sore muscles for a moment.

"Dammer!" he says. "Gonna have to take care of this broken back tonight. Getting too old to be doin' this alone." He tosses a posthole digger, wheelbarrow and shovel into the back of an ancient pickup truck. Before getting into the truck to drive home, he leans against the tailgate to take in the sunset.

A red sliver of sun slips below the edge of the farmland. The radio in the truck is on, and a voice comes through the static singing, "All my rowdy friends have settled down." The last hints of daylight give way to the deep dark of the countryside.

"Better git," Len mutters and heads to the driver's side door of the truck. He reaches for the door handle and stops suddenly. He stands perfectly still, his hand frozen in mid-air. Unable to move his arms or legs, his eyes roll around wildly in an effort to avoid two amber-colored beams of light coming from the pasture. The beams are fine and sharp, like lasers, and are directed into each of his eyes.

For a while, Len resists and continues moving his eyes every which way. As his eyes move, the beams move respectively with them, aiming for the dilated pupils. Soon, he becomes weary of resisting and looks directly into the light. The amber beams quickly bore into each pupil and carve deep into the eyeballs.

The light enters the optic nerves and from there travels to the brain and other nerve centers. At that moment, Len is loosed from paralysis, and a chilling scream gushes out of him. The scream lasts only until Len's seizure-like jerking stops and Len collapses to the ground, a heap of lifeless tissue and fluids.

As Len lay dead in the dirt with smoldering eye sockets staring blindly at the star-filled sky, his wife Amy paces at home, wondering why her husband is so late. At the same time, a sleek, black triangular object rises from the pasture and glides away into the night, carrying Len Wilkins' consciousness inside a small, luminous cylinder.

#

"Hey, Mom!" Riley Jensen yells as she walks in the front door of a Victorian-style house. She tosses aside some books on a bench in the vestibule and hurries down the hall, side-stepping into the kitchen long enough to grab a few chips from a bag on the counter. "Hey, Mom! Did you hear about Len Wilkins?" Riley says as she turns her head side to side and looks in each bedroom for her mom, Cece.

"I'm in here," Cece says. Cece turns off the light in the laundry room and steps into the hall. "Be right ... Oh! You scared the crap outta me!" she says, bumping into Riley and dropping a batch of freshly folded towels.

"Sorry, Mom," Riley says while stooping down to pick up the towels. "But have you heard about what happened to Mr. Wilkins?"

"Yes. I have," says Cece. "I guess Amy's a real mess. We're going to have to make something to take her." Cece sniffles and wipes her eyes. "Anyway," she says, "did you hear anything about the way it happened?"

"No," Riley says, "only some theories floating around school. Poor Len. He was so nice. Exactly what happened to him?"

"Well, I'm sure it's going to get around, so I'll tell you," says Cece. "Lenny's eyes were missing when they found him, kind of burned right out of his head, like a hot piece of metal was poked into his eyeballs and turned them to ash. Nothing else seemed to be wrong with him, but the coroner ordered an autopsy to try to find out what did this to him.

"I guess you haven't heard about this, either. There have been reports about people all over the Midwest being found dead, just like Len. People in rural areas and around small towns, like ours, found dead with their eyeballs burned out. I don't know what kind of sick weirdo would do that to people, but we're going to be very careful in this family," Cece says definitively as she caresses her pregnant belly.

"I don't know what to make of it," Riley says, "except some talk about people getting jacklighted."

"What?" asked Cece.

"Jacklighted," Riley replies. "It's something poachers do to kill deer. They drive around at night looking for deer. When they see one, they shine their headlights in its eyes to stun it and get an easy kill, with the deer at a real disadvantage.

"The story's spreading at school that some sickos are going around jacklighting, not deer, but people. The story, at least according to Jason Easton, is that they catch people alone at night, blind 'em with a laser or something and then murder them. I don't know. What do Dad and Grandpa make of all of this?"

"I haven't talked to either one of them much about it yet," says Cece. "We'll have to see what they think. In this case, Jason Easton may be right, but he's what, almost nineteen? And you're only fifteen. If you're getting ideas about him, don't. He's too old for you. In the meantime, you're not to be out and about at night at all. You come straight home from school every day, and I'll drive you where you want go. Deal?"

Riley pauses. "Deal," she finally says, but as she's saying it, she has an image of herself riding in Jason Easton's car, cruising the countryside on the outskirts of the quiet burg of Silverton looking for anything unusual. She quickly dismisses the image, and her thoughts turn to her grandpa, who lives alone about eight miles out of town on Newburg Road. It's hard for Riley not to worry about him, considering what happened to Len Wilkins.

#

"Gramps?" Riley says when Murray Jensen

answers the phone.

"Yes, darling. It's me. Who else would it be?" Murray lets out his characteristic chuckle.

"Well, you could have been an alien from outer space, the way you sounded." She giggles, then hesitates. "Grandpa, I just wanted to make sure you're OK after what happened to Mr. Wilkins."

"Yes, yes, I'm OK," he says, feigning annoyance at her concern. "I've heard this stuff's going on all over the place. I hope they get the devils who are doing it. That's all I can say, except to tell you, little girl, to be careful. And don't worry about me. I'll be fine."

"Well, Gramps, since you are so prehistoric and refuse to have a cell phone, no one can get hold of you when they need to, so you've got to make a deal with me: I'll bring you a phone, and you'll take it with you when you leave the house."

"You might be trying too hard to teach an old dog new tricks, baby doll," Murray says, laughing.

Riley cuts him off. "No, Grandpa! This is different. Maybe you should just come and stay with us in town for a while."

"Oh, no. I couldn't do that."

"So, you'll take the phone and carry it with you?"

"OK, sweetheart. I'll do it for you."

"All right, Grampulous. Mom and I will be out there later." There is another pause. "Gramps, have you ever heard of jacklighting?"

"Yeah. Cowardly poachers do it. They blind deer with their headlights and slaughter 'em. Why do you ask?"

"Oh, it's nothing. "Be seein' ya. Love ya."

"Yeah, yeah. Bye, now." Riley hangs up, relieved that Murray has agreed to accept the phone but feeling also this is only one hurdle she will face.

Cece thinks Riley's idea to give Murray a cell phone is a good one, so they drive out to the farm and get him set up. He agrees to keep the phone with him when he's outside and away from the house. Satisfied, Cece and Riley drive back home. "Oh!" says Cece as they turn off Newburg Road. "Feels like some little dude in my tummy might be thinking it's about time to come out. Call your dad for me. Make sure he gets home early in case we have to go to Decapolis."

Brant Jensen is pulling into the driveway as Cece and Riley drive in. He goes and opens the door for Cece. "Oh, Ooooooo," she moans as she tries to get out of the car. "I think we need to go to the hospital now, Brant!" Brant wastes no time helping Cece around to the passenger seat of the car.

"C'mon, Ri. Let's go," Cece says.

"Oh, Mom. I don't know what to do. I have a terrible feeling. I don't want Gramps to be out there alone. I, I need to get him to come here," says Riley, leaning against the car door.

"Well, we don't have time to argue about it," Cece says, exasperated.

"Just go call him!" says Brant as he begins to back out of the drive. "Tell him I said to come over."

"Go now!" Cece says. "Call Gramps. And then, Riley Marissa Jensen, you stay inside until he comes over or we get back!"

#

Riley would never forget the look of fear and perplexity in her mom's eyes as her parents drive off. That look makes Riley feel so strange and sad that she wishes for a moment she had gone with her parents. She watches them drive away until they turn the corner at the end of the block, then goes inside and dials Murray's number.

There is no answer. Riley dials the cell phone. It rings six times and goes to voicemail. Riley tries both phones five times each. Murray is apparently outside without the cell phone.

"Darn it! That stubborn old man," Riley says as she hops in the driver's side of a 1975 station wagon her dad always leaves the key in. Keeping the old boat, as Cece calls it, in decent running shape, instead of retiring it, seems to be Brant's favorite hobby. Now, Riley feels relieved he hasn't gotten rid of it.

"Oh! What a piece of junk this car is!" Riley says after the car sputters and dies at the end of the drive. She gets out, lifts the hood and fiddles with the choke and sparkplug wires. She goes back and tries the ignition again and again. The car isn't going to start.

Riley goes into the garage and looks intently at Brant's Harley, his pride and joy. She wrestles with the decision to take it. "To heck with it!" she finally says and gets on the bike. She rolls it backwards out of the garage and turns it around. A touch of a button fires up the hefty engine, and Riley speeds off, forgetting to wear any eye protection.

On North Street, Silverton's main drag, she pulls up to the stop light and revs the bike's engine, which turns the heads of several long-haired patrons standing outside the local pub. At the last stop before leaving town, Riley is barraged by whistles and catcalls from Jason Easton and his friends, who loiter outside the store on the corner.

Riley turns onto Newburg road and opens up the bike, nervously checking and rechecking the progress of the sunset in the mirror, the Harley purring like a lion underneath her. "Ow! Oh!" she says along the way as bugs hit her face. "Oh, sh...," she starts to say as a bug goes in her mouth and gets stuck in her throat. This almost makes her wreck. The bike wavers as she slows down and pulls over to the side, where she vomits on the tarred surface of the road.

Looking back toward the west through watery eyes, Riley sees a sundog in the clouds. She loves sundogs and always considers it quite a privilege to see one, since they are rare. Her aunt Lu first told her about them. "A sundog follows the sun around like a good and loyal dog following its master. Sometimes when the master has gone to bed, the sundog lingers in the sky for a while, guarding the golden estate of the sun king as day drifts into night," Lu said once. This is the only time in her life Riley Jensen fails to stop and watch a sundog disappear into the evening sky.

"Grandpa," Riley whispers and cranks the throttle. Birds fly out of the fields on either side as she passes. Dried corn whizzes by in a brownish-yellow blur as the Harley eats up the road. Riley grimaces when insects smash into her face but does not flinch.

A glance in the mirror reveals only a pink ripple in the clouds. Daylight is slipping away like sand in an hour glass, slipping away, down to the last few grains, like lost hope through Riley's fingers.

Riley isn't used to riding what a lot of seasoned bikers would call a <u>mean</u> <u>machine</u> on a dark country road. She doesn't see the possum coming. It's right in front of her before she can react.

<u>Thump</u>, <u>thump</u>. Both wheels pass over the possum and leave it rolling on the road, where it comes to a halt, squirms around in a pool of blood and then dies with a series of twitches. Normally, Riley cries if any creature dies, even a mouse, but she pays no mind to the animal sacrificed to the tires of the bike and speeds on towards a house with a weathered green mailbox leaning beside the road.

The turn comes up so fast that Riley nearly misses

it. The back tire skids out in an arc, and the bike almost goes down, but she pulls through the turn and heads up a gravel driveway. A cloud of dust goes up in her wake while the Harley thunders in the silence of the countryside.

She parks the bike next to a walk that leads to the front porch, gets off and hurriedly puts down the kickstand. After taking a few running steps toward the porch, she hears a crash behind her. "Oh, no!" she cries before she even looks back to see her dad's pristine bike on its side. This incident just about breaks her, but she bites her lip, swallows her tears and runs for the front door.

#

"Gramps? Gramps?" Riley says, rushing through the living room, flipping on lights as she goes. "Gramps! Where are you?" she yells. Murray doesn't answer.

She goes into the kitchen and finds Murray's cell phone on the table amidst a clutter of newspapers and issues of <u>Scientific</u> <u>American</u>. When she turns to go out the backdoor, she brushes against a half-eaten can of tuna, the kind with oil. The tuna splatters all over Riley when it falls off the counter. She curses under her breath and flies out the screen door, which closes with a bang.

Riley is sure Murray must have heard the screen door slam. Then why is he standing in the middle of the yard, just staring at something? "Hey, space case!" says Riley, standing on the porch outside the back door. He doesn't acknowledge her. "Hey, Murray! What on Earth are you doing?" she says, although she can't remember ever calling him by his first name. She heads down the steps, peering into the twilight, her heart pounding with fear.

When she walks toward Murray, he doesn't move, but she thinks she hears him say, "Go," although it also sounds like a moan. She can't be sure, because at the same time, a horse whinnies. The horse is Nettles, a black mare that usually has a calm temperament. However, Nettles now seems very agitated and is starting to tug at the strap Murray holds firmly with one hand.

Murray is standing there, still as stone, holding onto the horse. His jowls and lips quiver as he tries to speak, but he can't form any words. "Gramps! What the heck are you ...," she says but stops short when she sees Murray's eyes darting back and forth. Two amber-colored light beams are being focused into his eyes. Although unable to move any other part of his body, he moves his eyes around to keep from being blinded.

Riley looks in the direction Murray is facing and sees the origin of the lights in a clover field next to the house. She thinks of Len Wilkins and begins to tremble with terror for her grandfather. During the seconds she spends trying to process what's happening, Nettles begins to rare up and kick with her front legs, her hooves narrowly missing Murray as he stands paralyzed.

With a scream that is more like a battle cry, Riley springs towards Murray and drives into him, which knocks him off balance and sends him tumbling to the ground. The light beams follow his head to the lawn and lock onto his eyes again. Nettles begins neighing and kicking wildly, and Murray's head, now directly beneath her, is about to get a skull-crushing blow.

Although Riley is frantic, she acts in a composed manner. Her thinking is quick, her motions fluid and swift. She looks heroic as she leaps on Nettles' back and charges toward the clover field, her jet-black hair flying behind her.

Images of the Lone Ranger, Joan of Arc and other heroes might have come to Murray's mind had he seen Riley reign Nettles back and let her kick away at a triangular object that stands on a tripod. Murray would have watched in amazement as Nettles' steel-shoed hoof crushes the head of a grey-skinned creature wriggling on the ground beside the object.

He would have been devastated, however, to see the amber beams slice through Nettles' left front shoulder and cut her leg entirely off. Seeing Riley about to be thrown into the path of the beams would have brought sheer horror to Murray, but because he is temporarily blinded, he sees none of these events.

"Oh, Gramps," Riley says, bending down to help Murray get up. "You OK?"

"Yeah," says Murray, wheezing, "but I can't see too well." He looks at Riley and tries to focus. Eventually, she comes into a sort of blurred, kaleidoscopic view. He then turns toward Nettles, who kicks in pain on the ground. "Go into the house and get my gun out of the safe," he tells Riley.

"Oh no, Grandpa! We can't!" she cries.

"Yes, we can. We have to. Go get it!"

Murray gives Riley the combination to the safe, and within minutes, she returns with the gun. His eyesight clear once more, Murray looks toward the clover field and sees the amber beams are low to the ground and pointing in the opposite direction from them. He says, "Now! Go over there and help Nettles."

"I can't! I can't!" says Riley as a steady stream of tears flows down her face.

"You can, sweetheart. Don't think about it. Just do it for Nettles. I would, but I don't know if I can make it over there. Those lights made my knees wobbly. Please, go do it now, and be careful."

Riley goes to Nettles, who, wrenching in her own blood, struggles for each breath. Positioning herself so she won't be kicked, Riley looks into the mare's hazy eyes for a moment. "I'm sorry, girl," she says, sobbing. She then points the gun, looks away and pulls the trigger. The gun drops from her hand as she runs into her grandpa's arms.

"There, there. It'll be all right. We'll get through this," Murray says, patting Riley on the back as she hugs him. He lets her have a good cry and then wipes her eyes with a handkerchief he takes from the back pocket of his overalls. Riley feels ashamed that she wonders if Murray has actually used the hanky to blow his nose before drying her tears with it, instead of just being grateful he's alive.

"Did you get a good look at anything over there?" Murray asks.

"Yes. There's a black, triangle-shaped thing with those lasers coming out of it ... and some kind of creature. It's dead, I think." Murray's eyebrows raise. "Nettles killed it," Riley continues. "But I'm not sure. That light almost killed you, and it's what hurt Nettles. We have to disable it."

"I know. C'mon. We've got some work to do."

#

Riley follows Murray into a metal building with an end loader parked inside. She climbs up on the machine and squeezes into the cab with him. The tractor starts with a bang and rumbles slowly toward the black object. Murray poises the bucket over the object and lowers it with crushing force. As the object succumbs to the pressure, the beams emitting from it flicker on and off like amber lightening, then stop.

Murray wheels the machine around and digs a deep pit in the clover field. He sets the bucket down beside Nettles and uses it to nudge her gently into the pit. Murray and Riley both weep as he pushes dirt over the beautiful mare's body.

"You stay here," says Murray as he climbs off the end loader. "I'm going to check things out."

"No, Gramps. I'm scared, and I want to see it too."

"OK," he concedes. "Just stay behind me. We don't know anything about this."

The black object is crushed, its tetrahedral shape distorted beyond recognition. It emits a wisp of dark smoke that makes Murray cough. "I said stand back!" he says, holding his hand up behind him as Riley approaches. "Let's get rid of this first and then deal with <u>that</u> <u>thing</u>."

He points toward the grey humanoid being lying on the ground. Its skull is broken. It appears to be dead. Nevertheless, intermittent flashes of red light in its one uncrushed eye make Murray dubious about its true state of animation.

"What do you think it is, Gramps?" Riley asks.

"I don't know, but I know it's not from this world. And I know it was malicious and that I don't ever want to see anything like it again."

"But what do you think it was after?"

"I doubt we'll ever know that, but it will be best just to bury it," Murray says.

"I wonder where it's from," says Riley.

Murray motions toward the sky with a sweeping gesture. "See all those stars? You could almost take your pick as to which one it's from. But you might begin by taking a look at the Gliesian solar system."

"The what?"

"The Gliesian system. It's one of the nearest systems to ours with planets that might support life."

"I wonder if the creature had a name," Riley says. Murray doesn't answer. He doesn't know the creature is actually from the planet Gliese 581 g and that the being, whose name is Unceros, was dispatched to Earth with a hundred other Gliesians, or grays, as they are known, to deploy the device that caused Len Wilkins' demise.

They get back in the end loader and dig two more pits. Murray uses the tractor's bucket to push the black object, the tripod and all the dirt around it into one of the pits, then fills the hole with soil. He then scoops up the limp corpse of the being and dumps it into the second pit. As he fills in the pit, Riley wonders why he doesn't just put the object and the creature into one hole, but she's sure he has his reasons.

Murray parks the end loader, and they get out. "I think we better get going," he says. "But first I want to thank you for saving my tail back there." He reaches out and pulls her tight to him.

Riley doesn't respond to this overture but asks, "What about dad's bike?"

"Don't you worry about that now. I'll drive it home. You take my truck." He tosses her some keys. "I'll check it out tomorrow. If there's any damage, I'll get it fixed. If I'm staying with you for a day or two, I'll need something to do." He chuckles.

"About what happened here, what we saw and did," he says. "It's going to a take a while to soak it in. Wouldn't you think it best if we just didn't tell anyone about this right now, unless we think it would keep them out of harm's way to know about it?"

"Yes, Gramps. I agree. With a new baby hopefully coming home, we don't need to be stirring up any panic." She looks nervously toward the clover field. "I'm sure we'll see plenty of that soon enough with this kind of weird stuff going on.

"But Gramps, you were almost jacklighted. Those creatures are the jacklighters," she says thoughtfully. "That's got to be what killed Len Wilkins."

"I know," says Murray.

"Why do you think the laser beam cut off Nettles' leg but didn't blind you or burn out your eyeballs like Mr. Wilkins'?"

"I don't know. I guess the thing had just focused on me when you came up. Had me paralyzed, it did. I kept trying to keep it from shining in my eyes, but I was losing, kiddo, when you tackled me. Must have been that the creature controlled the intensity of the beams so they didn't blind me at first, until they'd done their dirty work, whatever that would have been. But then, when you and Nettles went racing up to it, it must have turned the lasers up to full tilt and sliced poor Nettles' leg clean off." He hangs his head for a moment and then says, "Time to go."

Riley jumps into Murray's truck and drives off with Murray following close behind on the Harley. As they drive into Silverton, everything seems normal. There are no signs of aliens with blinding lasers or anything like that. The antithesis of the setting strikes Riley as very strange as she goes down her block. She and Murray have just gone through otherworldly hell, and here is Silverton, quiet, quaint and peaceful as usual.

The only car in the drive is the station wagon. "Let's get the wagon up here," Murray says after he parks the bike in the garage. With Riley steering and pushing from the driver's side while Murray pushes from the back end, they get the car in its place, thinking it would be better not to have to answer any questions about why it has been moved.

They go inside the house. Riley goes into the bathroom and cleans up while Murray whips up some salad and cold cut sandwiches. They eat without speaking, then Murray goes to take a shower.

While Murray's busy, Riley sits in the quiet at the kitchen table. Looking out the windows into the dark makes her feel uneasy, so she shuts the blinds. The phone on the wall rings. "Hello," Riley says.

"Hey, Ri," says Brant on the other end. "We've got a little whippersnapper to bring home!"

"Whipper whater?"

"A boy, silly! You've got a baby brother!"

"That's amazing, Dad," she says, but as she says it, she feels the heavy weight of certainty that this little boy has come into a very dangerous world. "When will I get to see him? Tonight?"

"No. I don't think so. He didn't come naturally." Riley knows what that means. "So, he and your mom are going to be in here a little while."

"Ok. May I talk to Mom?"

"Maybe later. She's resting. See if Gramps will bring you here tomorrow. I'll call school so you can take the morning off. By the way, did you get that old coot to come?"

"Yes. I did. He's here now. I think, I'm hoping, he's going to stay here for a bit."

"All right, babe. Love you. Goodnight."

"Night, Dad. Love you too, and tell Mom and the baby that too."

#

The next morning Riley rides with Murray to the hospital to see her brother Arden. She coos at him and kisses his tiny fingers. "Hey, little fella," she says, "you look so intelligent. There's a lot behind those shiny, little eyes. The way your eyes look, I think you might just be a star child. That's it," she whispers, lightly touching the tip of Arden's nose with her finger. "You're a star child, come to brighten our home while the world outside turns dark."

About the Writer

Bill Knorr is a former English teacher and environmental professional who loves composing and recording music, drawing, painting, and writing young adult short stories. He has written over twenty short stories and one novella, all in the Young Adult/Science Fiction/Fantasy genre. From the Midwest, Bill draws much of his inspiration from small town or rural customs and characters. Many of his story ideas have come while hiking in some of the vast and beautiful forested areas of Illinois.

Bill's day gig is now primarily as a freelance technical copywriter, but he has also been delving into the realm of voice acting. Although much of his work experience has been in the industrial, environmental or educational fields, his true love is all things creative.

Short Story Press publishes short stories written by everyday writers. Visit www.ShortStoryPress.com to learn more.

Thank You

Thanks for getting this book!

Our ULTIMATE goal is to share our short stories to the world! We strongly believe that our publishing company is unique because we focus on unique and original short stories written by everyday people throughout the world. Our short stories are our small way of making a positive impact in the world by entertaining you, our Short Story Press reader to the fullest with our Short Story Press stories.

To help get the word out, your honest reviews and feedback are greatly appreciated. So after you have read this book, we'd like to ask you to take a quick moment to review the book. Thank you and we wish you all the best.

Thank you for your reviews online. We appreciate your honest reviews and feedback online. Thank you for being a Short Story Press reader. For more short stories, visit ShortStoryPress.com.

If you want to check out our non-fiction books, then check out our HowExpert guides at HowExpert.com.

To your success,

BJ Min
Founder & Publisher of Short Story Press
ShortStoryPress.com

Recommended Resources

- www.ShortStoryPress.com – Short Stories Written by Everyday Writers.
- www.HowExpert.com – Quick 'How To' Guides by Everyday Experts.

CPSIA information can be obtained
at www.ICGtesting.com
Printed in the USA
LVHW100552290322
714679LV00003B/73